by: Ian Wenstrand

Printed in the United States of America

First Printing, 2017

ISBN 978-0692958957

www.ianwenstrand.com
www. instagram.com/ianwenstrandart/

"C'mon, c'mon..." Sam stared up at the clock, wishing the next few hours of class away. Sitting at his desk, he eagerly anticipated the release of Endless Quest, the newest release from his favorite video game series. "This day is going to last forever," he grumbled.

Sam's mind drifted to the far-away castles and futuristic cities from his games. He fidgeted all day and doodled pictures of video game characters in his notebook. Sam had a video game obsession. After listening to his teacher lecture for what seemed like days, he picked up the very first copy of Endless Quest ever sold from the video game store on Main Street.

After picking up Endless Quest, Sam ran into his twin neighbors, Lucy and Leo.
"Hey Sam, what's the big hurry?" Lucy asked. "You should totally come skate behind the school with us. We found an awesome spot where the old playground is."

   Sam thought it sounded like fun, but someone was beckoning him to play the game. A voice in his head filled him with doubts, "You don't know them very well...you can't skate...you might fall." the voice said.

Sam was persuaded to play the game instead. A part of him wanted to go with, but someone was luring him home instead.

"No time Lucy, I have to find the Rusty Key to retreive the Ultimate Sword then defeat Gigas, the giant Golem."

Lucy looked bewildered, "Suit yourself, Sam, if you ever get done with that, come find us. It'll be fun!"

Sam used his usual shortcut through the alley to make it home in a flash.

Arriving home, Sam rushed upstairs and fired up his new game. In his haste, he neglected to read the warning in big red letters on the packaging: "DO NOT PLAY FOR EXTENDED PERIODS OF TIME." The warning didn't stop Sam from playing late into the night.

As usual, Sam's mother noticed a sliver of light creeping out from underneath his bedroom door.

"Sam!, It's way past your bedtime, and you have school tomorrow, turn off that game!"

"Ugh," groaned Sam. He turned the volume down to a whisper, placed a blanket at the foot of his door to block any light into the hallway, and kept playing. It was not like Sam to defy his mother, but the voice in his head had become even more controlling...

"Play!, play! Another level, you must never stop!" it commanded. Sam obeyed, and far exceeded the recommended time limit on the box.

The dancing pixels on
the screen mesmerized Sam.
Bleeps and bloops were all he
could hear. He was in a trance, but his
fingers continued to use the controller.

"Up, Up, Down, Down, Left, Right,..." he chanted
over and over as his hands frantically entered in the commands.

Pixels and polygons began trickling into the room. The last thing Sam
heard before becoming completely unconscious was the cackling that evil voice,
echoing in his head:

6

"Hahaha, Splendid work Sam!
We are finally free!"
The TV screen went dark, and Sam snapped
out of his daze. The game system was turned on,
but there was no graphics or sound. He decided to walk
outside and get some fresh air.
"Whew, that was the longest I've ever played!"
Opening the front door and stepping onto the front porch, he stood in awe at the
astonishing sight...

7

The game worlds were right at his doorstep. Sam's neighborhood was flooded with creatures and characters from his video game collection. The howl of the wind and the rustle of leaves were replaced by glitchy, 8-bit sound effects. Townspeople were in a panic as a smoldering volcano burst from the middle of the neighborhood. The quiet town was in absolute pandemonium.

Sam's street was being split apart by a river of red, molten lava. As he stood there in disbelief, the lava began to seep into a crevice on the porch. A loud "CRACK!" rumbled from behind Sam.

The porch beneath Sam's feet disconnected from his house and was swept up into the lava stream. Sam drifted west on the concrete slab, while his house drifted east toward Lily Lake. Floating along, Sam wondered what happened. "This is impossible!" he thought. "Am I dreaming?!".

He felt powerless as he traveled farther and farther away from home. The raft spun and swayed down the river until eventually, his house disappeared over the horizon. Up ahead was a more urgent problem: the lava was flowing rapidly over a soaring cliff, and Sam needed to jump off quick.

As he searched for a way off the raft, a large shadow descended overhead. Razor-sharp talons latched onto Sam's shirt as he began to lift into the sky.

★ LEVEL SELECT ★

The creature placed Sam safely away from the lava on the top of an ancient statue. As Sam turned to greet his rescuers, he was stunned to see who it was. "You...You're!...", uttered Sam. He stood in awe at the heroes whom he had just selected while playing Endless Quest.

" Greetings Sam, my name is Dusk, I hail from the game Endless Quest. This is my loyal companion, the dark dragon, Shade."

Of course, Sam knew this already. He'd explored villages and dungeons with the duo countless times before. "What's happening, how is this even possible?" Sam asked.

DUSK

Dusk began to explain: "Ultimo, the final boss of Endless Quest, has used you to link the real and virtual dimensions. He only needed someone to play the game long enough for him to finish casting his spell."

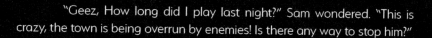

Sam

"Geez, How long did I play last night?" Sam wondered. "This is crazy, the town is being overrun by enemies! Is there any way to stop him?"

"We need more members in our party. Ultimo has teamed up with villains from the other games, and we'll need a team of our own to stand a chance against him. There are also super items scattered throughout the worlds that we must locate. Equipping these will give the team special abilities that we'll need to beat Ultimo. Finally, we need to reach the area where the portal between the two realms first appeared. Where was the last place you played the game?" Dusk asked.

"In my bedroom..." answered Sam. "...But my house..., my house is somewhere on the other side of town. The lava swept it away. It must be miles away by now."

"Then that is where we must go," said Dusk. "Severing the connection between the two dimensions is the only way to restore order. We must break Ultimo's spell, for if we wait too long, the world as you know it will cease to exist. Only the game world will remain"
"Sam, we need your help navigating the worlds. You are the only one with knowledge of both the real and virtual. Will you assist us on our journey?"

"I know it will be hard, but if there's even a small chance to fix things, I have to try." said Sam nervously.

Sam led them out of his neighborhood and onto a chaotic Main street. It had been overrun by evil robots from the game Robo Core War. Futuristic buildings from Neo-Japan had replaced the shops and businesses lining the road. Sam and Dusk spotted the game's cybernetic hero crouched behind a concrete barricade.

"Kid Robo's the name, you must be Sam. We'll need my Booster Boots before we can get past Main Street. Intel put the coordinates on my radar, it looks like they're on the basement level of that laboratory". Kid Robo said.

He pointed to the group's first level, where the video game store used to be. The maniacal Professor Hazard turned it into a research lab for his malevolent experiments.

"The enemies just keep re-appearing to guard the lab. We'd be fighting all day if we go through the front. There's no way in until they leave, and we don't have time to waste" Lamented Kid Robo.

Sam thought for a moment about another way in. He recalled the time he waited in line for the release of Fast Food Dudes. The video game store lets people who reserve the game in early through the basement door in the back. "Follow me," Sam said, "I can get us in."

They sprinted around back and entered through the secret basement door. Walking down a long corridor, through two gates, they became face to face with the Level One boss...

Professor Hazard was waiting for them in his mech-suit. It was Kid Robo's time to fight. He dashed and dodged his way past the Professor's drill punches and laser eyes. Sam knew the Professor's fight patterns and used that strategy to help Kid Robo.

After a flurry of charged shots from Kid Robo's blaster arm, the Professor's mech-suit was reduced to scrap metal. The booster boots were installed on Kid Robo, and the group continued on to the next level.

Leaving the laboratory, they caught a glimpse of Sam's home far away in the distance. "There's my house! It stopped at Lily Lake." Sam's house sizzled as the water from the lake mixed with molten rock. "The shortest route to Lily Lake is through a mountain path behind my school. I know a shortcut"

Sam's confidence grew as he guided them around the laboratory to the alley in the back. He used the route many times as a way to get home from school faster. This time, however, the brick walls were covered with graffiti, and the alley looked rougher than usual.

When the team stepped midway through the alley, they were suddenly confronted by a crowd of nasty-looking characters who were out looking for a brawl. The heroes were out-numbered on both sides. The rowdy crew began to close in when all of the sudden, they heard a loud commotion from further in: "CRUNCH! CRACK! BANG!".

It was Boomhilda from Super Button Smash II. As a warning to the street gang, she was demolishing an old car with her bare hands. Seeing her strength and might, the nasty crowd that confronted Sam quickly ran away. Without fighting anyone, Boomhilda cleverly defeated her foes.

"Me...Boomhilda. You call me Hilda. Hilda smash car. Me have Sam's back" she said in a thick Russian accent.

Sam nervously thanked her, and she decided to accompany them on their journey. As they left, Hilda found her super item: a pair of Power Gloves that the gang had dropped.

The group emerged from the alley, strengthened by the addition of Hilda. Her power and fighting technique were second to none. Everyone followed Sam to the rear of the school. As Sam turned the corner, the sky seemed to dim...

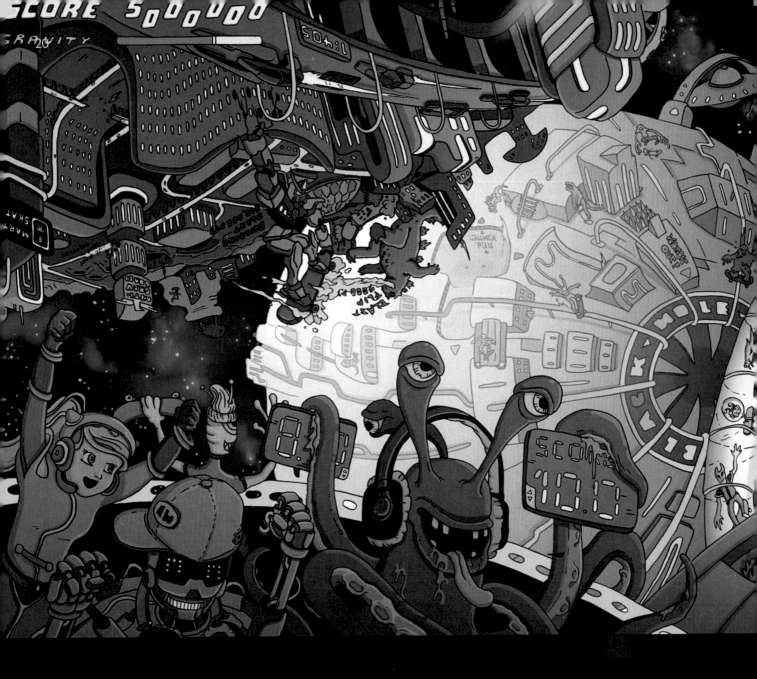

Planets were floating high above, and stars shimmered in the night sky. Down below, Sam saw strange alien lifeforms grinding neon rails and executing gravity-defying tricks. Gazing at the neon lights, Sam realized they had just stumbled into the game Galaxy Shredding. Streaking by him like a comet, Ollie, the inter-dimensional skateboarder welcomed Sam: "Yo Sam! Long time no see! Pound it!" an excited Ollie said as he bumped fists with Sam.

"I've been orbiting the area, trying to find some gnarly skate spots, but my radar is jammed because of the meteor shower. To win this contest, I need to find the most radical skate spot in the entire universe! Can you help me find it?"

Sam remembered the area where Lucy and Leo wanted to meet up with him - the old playground. Hidden behind some trees and packed with rails and ramps, the location was perfect for impressing the judges. Ollie landed countless combinations of stellar tricks, and with Sam's help, he racked up the highest scores in the galaxy!

      He won the contest and was awarded the prized Rocket board! The most tricked-out board in all the cosmos! Ollie decided to join Sam on his quest, in case there were any sweet skate spots along the way. Behind the school lay one more level on their path to Lily Lake, the treacherous Rift Mountains.

Everyone followed Sam to the path behind the school. The hills he was used to seeing were now towering mountains that plunged into the sky.

They trudged up the long and winding path. Ascending higher and higher, the team was hit with piercing winds and blinding snow. Unable to see through the blizzard, and being attacked by Evil Snowmen, everyone sought shelter in a nearby gemstone mine.

Shade started a small fire, and everyone warmed themselves by it. Crystals and precious stones peeked out from the walls, twinkling in the light of the fire. It was a welcome rest from the amount of climbing they endured. But they had to get moving soon, and they had no idea where to go.

Near the pit of the cavern, Sam noticed a small glimmer of light that became bigger and bigger until they were face to face with a new friend.

The winged pixie named Runa hailed from the game most fable. "Teeheehee..." She giggled at Sam and directed him to some shovels and pickaxes. Being a pixie, Runa only spoke in an ancient Fairy language, which mostly consisted of giggling and laughing.

She signaled for the group to dig in a certain patch of dirt. Runa was insistent that something special was buried underneath the rock and clay. After the team dug small holes everywhere in the cave, Ollie finally uncovered the final super item, the legendary Golden Boomerang for Runa.

By finding another member of their team, the group was reinvigorated and decided to make their way out of the mine.

Weaving in and out of tall trees, while braving the harsh winds, Tuva helped them navigate through the forest. Crossing the tree line at the bottom of the mountain, the bitter cold began to subside, and they proceeded towards Sam's house. Arriving at their destination, Sam stopped to soak in the vast beauty of their final level: Lily Lake.

25

The fishing lake was now a sweltering oasis with flowing waterfalls and lilypads swaying on the water. Surrounded by dense jungle, tropical animals and creatures Sam had only seen in the game Endless Quest peeked at them from the trees. Sam's house had slipped from the lava stream and hit landfall on an island near the middle of the lake.

"This is my homeworld," said Dusk. "Tread carefully, Ultimo could be lurking anywhere." The team moved through deep water and climbed on shifting land masses to traverse the level. Sam's house was just up ahead, but there was one enormous obstacle standing in their way...

"Woah, It's Gigas, the giant Golem," said Sam. The massive stone beast firmly stood guard and surrounded Sam's house. Kid Robo used his Booster Boots to push him, but the Golem would not budge. Hilda put on her Power Gloves and tried to lift the giant's leg, but it was too heavy. Ollie crashed into him with his Rocket Board, but the slumbering beast would not be moved. Runa used her magical Golden Boomerang to knock Gigas from his post, but he stood motionless.

"We need to find a way in!" yelled Sam. The virtual and real worlds were almost entirely merged, and the team was out of ideas. "Hahaha!" cackled a sinister yet familiar voice.

Ultimo, the evil sorcerer, stood perched like a crow on the shoulder of his minion, Gigas. Hearing Ultimo laugh, Sam remembered exactly what happened to him when he was playing the game earlier: "He was the voice in my head!" Sam thought.

"You cannot move Gigas the immovable! He is immune to all magic and physical attacks! You will never enter, and very soon I will become ruler over all the worlds. Hahaha!" As the menacing Ultimo laughed, game villains emerged from hiding to attack the heroes.

"Sam, you must find a way in and sever the connection to the game world. It's the only way to restore order to the realms!" Yelled Dusk as he defended himself against Ultimo. The Heroes had their hands full.

Even though Ultimo was the one who put a spell on him, Sam realized how much time he was actually spending playing video games. Much like the golem, when Sam played video games, he wouldn't budge for anything.

"How can I get the golem to move?" Sam thought.

Remembering the Port-a-Play he always kept in his pocket, an idea struck Sam. He wondered if the giant would go for a round of his favorite puzzle game, Mineral Dig.

"He might get bored just standing there, what's a better distraction than video games?"

Sam pulled out the Port-a-Play and turned on Mineral Dig. He oriented the warm glow of the screen to face the giant and turned the volume up as loud as it could go.

The Golem's eyelids slowly raised as the game caught its attention. It lumbered down to the Port-a-Play and began to mash the buttons. Sam's trick had worked! The giant was distracted.

Sam climbed on top of the golem and tumbled through his front door. He sprinted upstairs and clutched the cord to his game system. As Sam began to pull, he heard the voice in his head once again...

"Don't do it, Sam, you'll lose your new friends, you can't beat the bad guys." Sam hesitated as cords began to wrap around his legs and arms.

"Pull the cord, Sam! It must be done!". Dusk shouted. Sam looked out the window and saw Dusk keeping Ultimo at bay.

Sam shook the doubts from his head. With his new-found confidence, he broke Ultimo's spell, and was able to think for himself again. Sam nodded in agreement toward Dusk and yanked the cord from the wall.

"VOOOOOOSSHHHH!!" The virtual worlds started to swirl back into their games.

"NOOOOO!" yelled Ultimo as he was sent back to his world. Ultimo and the other villains were transported to their respective games once more.

Sam exhaled a sigh of relief as Dusk and the other heroes ran upstairs to his bedroom.

THANK YOU
FOR PLAYING!

"Thank you, Sam," said Dusk. "We will soon return to our games as well. The rest of the world will not remember what happened today and all that is virtual will go back from whence it came. We are indebted to you. As a gift, please accept any of our super items for your own. This is the only object that will remain from the virtual realm. You can use it to remember us by." Sam thought for a bit and picked out an item.

"You can still see us when you pop in a game though!" said Kid Robo. "Hilda miss Sam." sniffled Hilda. "Teeheehee..." Runa giggled.

The heroes waved goodbye and were transported safely back to their homeworlds. With everything seemingly back to normal, Sam laid down in his bed, exhausted from his adventure.

The next morning, he woke up to find his game system fried. Sam's parents explained that a tornado wrecked their town and wiped out all the power. Through the window, Sam could see wreckage and debris everywhere.

Walking onto what used to be his front porch, he saw Lucy and Leo rolling down the street on their skateboards. Lucy waved and shouted. "School's closed Sam! There's a bunch of holes in the roof and huge craters on the sidewalk. They had to shut it down. Leo and I are going skating. Are you in?!" shouted Lucy.

As the twins talked to Sam, the voice feeding Sam with doubts was gone. Sam smiled at Lucy, grabbed his new Rocket Board, and said:

"I'm game."

56120601R00022

Made in the USA
San Bernardino, CA
08 November 2017